FOUR BAD UNICORNS

To my sister, Susanna, who was The Wall
in so many tents and castles.

First published in Great Britain in 2022 by Andersen Press Ltd.,
20 Vauxhall Bridge Road, London SW1V 2SA, UK.
Vijverlaan 48, 3062 HL Rotterdam, Nederland
Copyright © Rebecca Patterson 2022.
The right of Rebecca Patterson to be identified as the author
and illustrator of this work has been asserted by her in accordance
with the Copyright, Designs and Patents Act, 1988.
Printed and bound in China.
1 3 5 7 9 10 8 6 4 2
British Library Cataloguing in Publication Data available.
ISBN 978 1 83913 103 5

FOUR BAD UNICORNS

Rebecca Patterson

Andersen Press

Since August we've gone **UNICORN CRAZY!**

There's Frankie, my big sister, doing a

BIG UNICORN YAWN!

And here's me, Connie! With Daddy doing my rainbows and Frankie doing my unicorn socks.

Frankie can eat her cereal in fourteen seconds! That's top unicorn speed. But Daddy is so slow feeding me. And last Saturday me and Frankie were in a massive rush to play...

UNICORN FARMERS! OUR BEST GAME EVER!

But then the doorbell went.

It was those Beswicks from next door.
Both of them.
They wanted to come in and play.

Straight away Ada Beswick said, "Everyone knows there's no such thing as Unicorn Farmers! We have to make a Unicorn Palace of Wonder!"

And I had to be part of the wall.

Then Ada said, "**WALLS DON'T MOVE!**

You can be a sleeping unicorn with little Colin and I will be Queen of Unicorns in my Throne of Rolling Power.

And give me the twinkle high shoes,
Frankie, because you're just a unicorn.
Now all you unicorns have to dance!

DANCEY PRANCEY!"

Then Ada got mad with us.

"This is very **BAD** unicorn dancing. I will put all of you in my **UNICORN PRISON!**"

Which was no fun for anybody.

So we bashed down the walls.

I yelled, "And we're escaping on our Bad Unicorn Train!"
And Ada yelled, "No! That's not a proper unicorn train!
There's **NO SPARKLES!**"

"Bad unicorns don't have sparkles!" I said.

"Wait for me!" she shouted. "I can't run in the twinkle shoes! I'm in charge and I'm The Unicorn Queen!"

So I yelled back, **"BAD UNICORNS DON'T CARE!"**

But then the Unicorn Queen...

wailed, "You are **VERY BAD UNICORNS** and I don't want to be your **QUEEN!**"

Colin said, "But you were a bad queen, Ada."
Frankie said, "Oh, we've all been **BAD UNICORNS.**"
And I said, "So now let's be good
unicorns together!"

And we flew that unicorn train back to Unicorn Land and had a big unicorn party. It didn't stop till the Beswicks had to go home for lunch.

After lunch Frankie and I played Unicorn Farmers till tea and Unicorn Holidays till bed.

"Those Beswicks are good at unicorns," said Frankie. "Not as good as us!" I said. "Us two are the best." "Too right!" whispered Frankie. "We're the All Powerful Queen Sisters of The **UNICORN UNIVERSE.**"

"Yes!" I said. And that night we were.